Ambrose and the Princess

Margo Sorenson

illustrated by
Katalin Szegedi

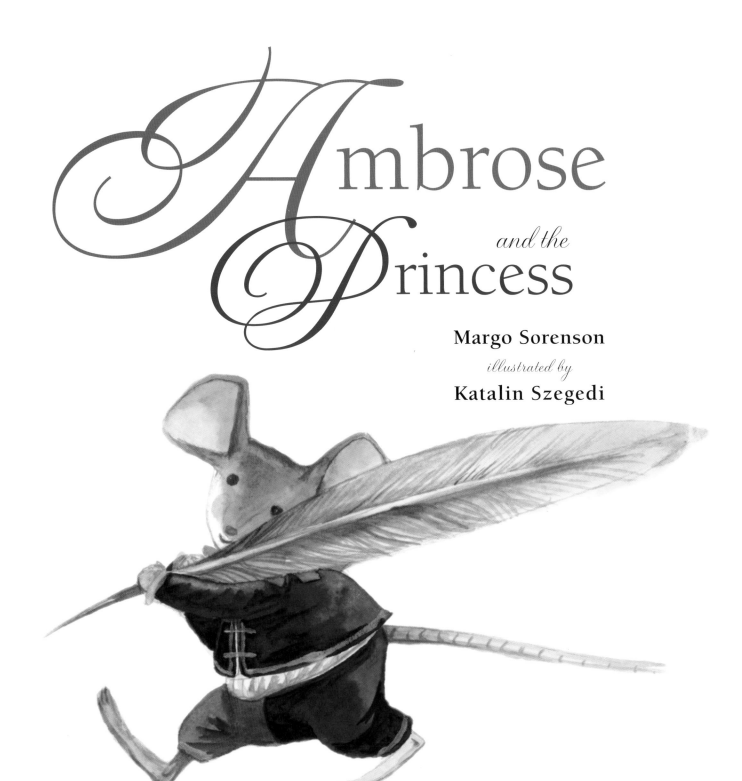

Ambrose the Mouse

LITURGICAL PRESS
Collegeville, Minnesota

www.litpress.org

mbrose scampered into the cathedral with his mouse cousins and skidded to a stop.

"Look!" Ambrose exclaimed. He stared at the green boughs and garlands decorating the cathedral. "It really looks like Christmas, doesn't it?"

Cousin Emma smiled at him.

"Yes, Ambrose, Christmas," Simon joked. "You're a genius."

"Ambrose daydreams so much he forgot it was Christmas!" Cedric said.

"Now, cousins," Grandpa scolded, "it *is* Christmas. Be loving."

Ambrose sighed. His cousins had too much fun teasing him—except for Emma.

"Line up!" Grandma called. Ambrose wriggled into line next to Emma. "You know our mouse family has always been a very important part of the cathedral."

All the cousins nodded.

"We work hard to help the bishop and all who worship here," Grandpa said. "We may be small, but we can make a difference. Because we're little, we are able to pay attention to the small things. That's our talent—and how we can help people. Remember how special we feel when we can use our talent to make others happy?"

"I hope all of you have been paying attention to the small things," Grandma said.

Uh-oh, Ambrose thought, looking down at the stone floor. He would pay more attention, he promised himself. He wanted to help too!

Grandpa looked solemnly at all the mice. "Sometimes the answer to helping someone is right under our noses."

"Ah-choo!" Ambrose sneezed. The greenery was tickling his nose. The cousins snickered.

"All the city folk will come to the cathedral tonight for Christmas Eve Mass. Peasants and merchants will come. Even the new princess, Princess Eleanor, will be here," Grandma announced. "Pay attention to the little things, so that you can help someone."

"The princess! Maybe I can help the princess," Ambrose whispered to Emma.

Emma patted Ambrose.

"How could the princess need help?" Emma asked.

"Even princesses can use some help," Grandpa said. "The bishop says nothing here seems to make her happy."

Ambrose and Emma exchanged glances.

That night, dozens of people thronged through the cathedral's huge doors. The silversmiths, the coopers, and the tailors ushered in their children. The merchants and peasants brought their families. With her nuns, the abbess from the convent led in the small, wide-eyed girls from the convent school. The little girls giggled and poked at each other. The abbess frowned and shushed, but they only giggled more.

Ambrose smiled and whispered to Emma, "It looks as if the abbess needs help, too."

Emma nodded.

The Princess Eleanor, wearing a red, fur-trimmed mantle, entered the cathedral.

A hush fell over the worshipers. Ladies-in-waiting, a priest, and servants followed the princess.

The little schoolgirls stared at the princess. She smiled at them, and they ducked their heads.

The Mass began. Ambrose saw the princess looking peaceful during the prayers and the chants. But after the bishop gave the final blessing, her smile faded.

Ambrose grabbed Emma's paw.

"We have to hear what the princess says," he urged. The rest of the cousins raced after them.

The bishop greeted the princess.

"Your Highness, we are grateful for all you give to the convent school and to the poor," the bishop said. "In the brief time that you have been here, you have been so generous to everyone."

"Thank you," Princess Eleanor said, softly.

"I hope this Yuletide will bring you happiness," the bishop added.

The princess sighed. "You are kind. I like it here, but . . . something is missing. I am going on a long journey soon. Maybe then I can find something to do that will make me happy."

The bishop shook his head. "We will miss you," he said.

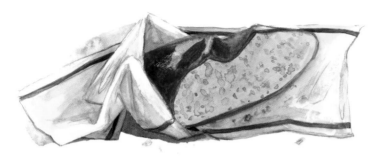

"*I* want to find out what she can do *here* that will make her happy!" Ambrose exclaimed to Emma.

Grandma said, "Ever since she came on Michaelmas, the princess has been sending firewood, clothing, and bread for the poor each week. She gives silver to the convent school and to the church. If she leaves, many people will miss her."

"I don't want her to go either!" Ambrose exclaimed. "*I* will help her want to stay," he said to Emma.

"Remember," Emma whispered to Ambrose. "Grandpa said that the answer could be right under your nose!" She giggled.

Ambrose wiggled his nose. "I'll make a plan," he said. Emma squeezed his paw.

The next day, Christmas Day, Ambrose and Emma burrowed in some hay left for the horses outside the cathedral doors.

"Here comes the cart from the castle," Ambrose said, "with bread and wood and clothes for the poor."

"What will you do?" Emma asked.

Ambrose smiled. "I'll wait till the carter is ready to return to the castle. I'll hide inside the cart and ride along. I'll follow the princess all day," he said. "I'll try to pay attention to the small things to see what might make her happy."

Emma squeaked, "What if a horse squashes you? What if one of the castle cats . . . ?"

Ambrose straightened his shoulders. "I'll be all right," he said. "When I come back, I'll have the answer to helping the princess." Ambrose swallowed hard. He hoped so.

His heart beating fast, Ambrose scrambled up the wooden wheel of the cart and dove in. All during the bumpy ride to the castle, Ambrose sat quivering in the cart. Was he doing the right thing?

The cart pulled over the drawbridge, through the iron gates, and into the castle courtyard. Children ran by, laughing, and servants and craftsmen hurried to their work.

Ambrose scrambled down from the cart.

Where was the princess? Her morning Mass would be over. Ambrose scurried up the stairs and into the Great Hall.

Garlands and green boughs for Christmas decorated the hall. Ambrose's pink nose whiffled at the smells of roast duck, poached haddock, and pork spiced with cinnamon and cloves.

Knights and ladies sat at linen-covered tables with silver plates and cups. The princess sat at a high table, her back to the huge blazing hearth. Her ladies-in-waiting talked and giggled around her, but her friends' chatter didn't make her laugh. She fed a little dog some scraps and smiled, but just for a moment.

The servants rushed back and forth, but none of them asked the princess what dishes to serve next. Ambrose watched the princess, but all the delicious food didn't make her smile.

The sounds of musicians' lutes and pipes began. A juggler worked magic with golden balls, while the princess watched. A clown asked riddles, and knights and ladies guessed at the answers and laughed. When they all finished, Princess Eleanor paid everyone with silver pennies, but her eyes didn't sparkle for long.

Ambrose frowned. What could the princess do that would make her happy?

A commotion! The princess stood up. Where was she going? Scampering across the rush-covered floor, Ambrose raced through the crowd, dodging dozens of feet shod in leather and boots.

Aha! Ambrose squirted around the gilt chair leg and climbed up into the princess's silken purse. He squeezed his eyes shut. Thud! Ambrose landed in the bottom. Now he could be with the princess all day.

"Ah-choo!" he sneezed. Something tickled his nose. A feather? Yes— a quill pen. Sheets of vellum with writing rustled next to him.

"A red, red rose smells so sweet to the nose," he read, squinting in the dark. Poetry! The princess wrote poetry?

Suddenly Ambrose felt the bag being lifted into the air. He felt dizzy, swinging back and forth.

Then, Ambrose heard horses neighing and birds calling. Hawking! The Princess Eleanor was going to fly her trained hawks in the woods.

Ambrose shuddered. The first thing a hawk would love to find would be a little plump mouse! He'd have to be careful, or Emma would have one less mouse cousin.

Ambrose pulled himself up and poked his head out.

The princess untied her hawk, and the bird soared into the air. Ambrose ducked behind the princess. He didn't need to be the falcon's next meal!

"Look!" the princess exclaimed. "Isn't it beautiful?"

Wouldn't hawking make the princess happy? Ambrose's heart lifted.

"I'll bring the hawk in, Your Highness" the head falconer said. "That is my task."

A little shadow crossed the princess's face. No, Ambrose sighed. Hawking wasn't the answer.

After the ride, the horses stabled, Ambrose thudded and thumped in the bottom of the princess's purse as she climbed flights of stairs. Where were they going? Suddenly, Ambrose felt himself dumped on a soft cushion. He peeked out and saw the princess seated at a chessboard.

"Checkmate," the princess said quietly, after moving a bishop and knights.

Ambrose jumped. Surely she'd be happy about winning at chess?

"I like to use the knights' moves to checkmate, too," one of the ladies-in-waiting said.

"Of course," Princess Eleanor gently answered, as she left the chessboard and picked up a lute.

The liquid notes of the lute rang out as the princess plucked the strings.

"I know that tune also," one of her friends announced.

Princess Eleanor smiled. "How nice," she answered, and she put the lute away.

"I must go and tend to the business of the castle now," she said.

Ambrose jounced along in the bottom of the purse as the princess made her way down stairs.

In the castle kitchen, the princess spoke to the cook.

"There's no need to trouble yourself here, Your Highness," the cook said. "I have made sure the kitchen is all in order."

The princess greeted the housekeeper in the laundry.

"Of course all the linens are mended and clean, and the plate is polished, Your Highness," the housekeeper said. "I've already taken care of everything."

Next, the princess met with the bailiff in his rooms.

"Your Highness, I have dealt with all the peasants' rents and the crops to plant. You don't need to worry," the bailiff said, putting away the records in a cabinet.

Ambrose heard the princess sigh a little sigh. He frowned.

The sun was sinking. He had to go home to the cathedral. What would he tell everyone?

"I still have to find what will make the princess want to stay," Ambrose said bravely to Emma, when he got home. "What can the princess do that will make her happy?" he asked. Emma patted him.

Days passed. Every day, Ambrose puzzled over everything that had happened with the princess at the castle.

Grandma and Grandpa said that paying attention to the small things was his talent. But what were the small things he needed to see? Ambrose wondered. And Grandpa kept saying the answer could be right under his nose. Ambrose wiggled his nose again and sighed.

The morning of Epiphany dawned, the Twelfth Day of Christmas!

"Ah-choo!" Ambrose sneezed as he and Emma scurried into the cathedral for Mass.

"The princess will come," Emma whispered. "I hope it won't be the last time."

"Ah-choo!" Ambrose sneezed again. The garlands and greenery were tickling his nose. "Ah-choo!" The greenery tickled his nose even more than the princess's feather pen in her purse!

Worshipers began coming into the cathedral. Ambrose watched the abbess and convent nuns ushering in their young schoolgirls, who whispered and giggled.

"Ah-CHOO!" Ambrose dabbed at his nose.

His nose! Right under his nose . . .

Ambrose's eyes widened. The princess's feather pen had been right under his nose, making him sneeze. He remembered the princess's poetry—that was her talent!

Ambrose stared at the wriggling schoolgirls. He blinked.

Yes! He had the answer!

Paying attention to the small things *was* his talent! Could he make it all work?

Ambrose grabbed Emma's paw. "Hurry!" he said.

"Hush!" the abbess said to the schoolgirls. The nuns shook their heads.

"They have to learn so much," the abbess murmured to the bishop. "I need help with them."

"I know!" Ambrose wanted to shout.

"The Princess Eleanor! She comes!" a voice said.

Ambrose took a deep breath.

He waited until the princess was right next to the abbess and the schoolgirls.

Now! he told himself.

Ambrose scampered into the center of the aisle.

"Eeeeek!" the princess cried out. Her silken purse fell from her grasp. "A mouse!"

In a flash, Ambrose tugged the quill pen and poems out of the bag and onto the floor in front of everyone. Then he fled under a bench, his heart thumping.

One of the little girls picked up a sheet. "Poetry!" she said. "The princess writes poetry!"

"Look!" said another. "A rose, a lovely rose . . ."

"Your Highness," said the abbess in surprise, "I didn't know you enjoyed writing poetry."

Princess Eleanor blushed the same deep rose color of her mantle.

"Perhaps," the abbess said, glancing at the rows filled with awe-struck schoolgirls, "you would agree to helping a little with the convent school and sharing your talent? The young girls could learn from you."

A smile wreathed the princess's face.

"I would be so happy to stay and help you teach the girls," Princess Eleanor said. "I could share my love of writing poetry with them! Thank you!"

"Yes!" Ambrose squeaked to his cousins. "I *knew* that the princess would be happy to use her talent to help others!" He winked at Emma. "Just like me!"

Emma clapped her paws together. The cousins cheered for Ambrose, and Grandma and Grandpa hugged him.

"Ambrose!" Emma said. "You found the answer to the princess's happiness—it really was right under your nose!"

"Ah-CHOO!" Ambrose sneezed, his ears turning pink.